D1595328

CIRCULATION

Circulation
Tim Horvath

SUNNYOUTSIDE
BUFFALO

Acknowledgments

"Circulation" won the 2006 Prize of the Society for the Study of the Short Story, judged by Clark Blaise. It was also a finalist in *Glimmer Train*'s Spring 2005 Short Story Contest for New Writers and in the 2007 St. Petersburg Summer Literary Seminars Contest.

Special thanks to Greg Horvath, who saw so many versions along the voyage.

ISBN: 978-1-934513-14-9

sunnyoutside
P.O. Box 911
Buffalo, NY 14207
USA
www.sunnyoutside.com

For My Parents
TO WHOM I OWE SO MUCH AND
WHOSE STORIES CONVERGE IN ME

When we were awash with youth, we were all led to believe that our father was assembling a book called *The Atlas of the Voyages of Things*, or as we shortened it, *The Atlas*. That it was eventually destined to enter the world was incontestable—one day, assuredly, we would march into the bookshop behind his gallant stride, and there, on the shelf, would sit the book, sprawling, coffee-table-ready, his name beaming from the front as on a theater marquee. "You see, boys?" he'd say, and we would solemnly nod.

But before you get overly swept away in such childhood reverie, I owe you a snapshot of him from years later, nearer the present: in a hospital bed, riggered to a set of machines that monitored many of his bodily functions. My memories of the strapping man I once knew—almost fiendish in his independence, wearing his learning like his plaid flannel at barbecues and on vacations, splitting hairs with the tour guide in an underground cave about this or that obscure fact—vied with the presence of the helpless man before me. His body itself had been extended through tubes into clear hanging bags—transparent, clearly labeled external organs. His body was being perpetually translated into the language of quantification, via feedback machines through which rates and levels looped again and again.

His body; his body. In such mantras, electronic and otherwise, I could achieve a semblance of peace. Amidst the faint hum of fluorescent lights and machines, an image would sometimes materialize for me of a brown-haired girl with a Hula-hoop. She was so adept and satisfied with its steady motion that she could gyrate it indefinitely. At some point in each of my visits, I arrived at some version of that peace, which came to stand, however fleetingly, for infinity. Those visits were frequent. I was trying to make up for the fact that

Aidan, my brother, was far away, and that when these rhythms reverted to silence, it would register barely a blip, I think, in my mother's day.

Seeing him so reduced, though, it was impossible not to think of *The Atlas* and the fervid energy it had once commanded. Behind the door of his office, which jutted proudly at the stern of our first house, overlooking the yard and taking in maddening sunsets, he was supposedly huddled amidst his papers in the evening hours, piecing together a masterwork, a lifelong enterprise. There was a certain comfort in glancing up on summer evenings while we built a fort at the edge of our yard where the woods began, with the volley of dogs barking back and forth nearby. It was the comfort of your tongue tripping on your own sweat, a friendly reminder that of the world's salt, a share is yours. His presence hovered over us.

For a long time, my brother Aidan and I had a rather comical misunderstanding of what an ordinary atlas actually was, our definition warped by what we were told about this book. We revealed this to each other years later, our own laughter backed by that of Aidan's family. His wife,

9

son, and daughter could not get over how "weird" we both were, daddy and "Silly Uncle Jay."

It was not our only failure of understanding. Until I was older—I couldn't pinpoint exactly when—I held intuitions about the nature of paper that would be considered by most profoundly strange. My father worked as an editor by day, and one of the perks of his job was the paper he would bring home for us to color or scrawl on, piles consisting of scrap-versions of manuscripts. One side of each page was still blank; on the "reverse" of each page was a smattering of text. Without even considering that it might be otherwise, I assumed that *paper itself* was one-sided. All things that could be said or drawn were thus built upon the backs of words already written: dancing constellations of musings on metaphysics, the mineral composition of scarabs, the origins of the treble clef. I am, of course, projecting backward with an adult's grasp of the world. At the time, they were simply the "wrong" side of the page, bearing no more meaning than the dull gray backing of aluminum foil or the mineral deposits on the underbelly of a rock.

But atlases. Our misunderstanding was exacerbated by the constant references made to *The Atlas*. No occasion or gathering could take place without it being invoked. If my Uncle Gerry was in from Detroit, it was only a matter of time before my uncle would growl, "How's that book of yours coming?" his voice bearing its precarious mix of support and doubt like an overly full soup bowl.

"It's coming along great, Gerry," he'd say emphatically. "I tell you, though, I'm gonna need your help on the part about cars, you being up there in Detroit and all."

"Yes, but I'm a chemist, Gus," Gerry would shoot back.

"I *know* that, Gerry, but you're up there in Detroit and, well, by God, you're my man on assignment for those particular pages," my dad would insist.

Always, when asked about the status of the book, even as a form of small talk, my father would plead for the personal assistance of the person asking, making him or her feel, at least for a few moments, indispensable to the project. That included the guy at the corner store, our dentist, the fellow who checked our water meter. And through my child's eyes, they all seemed both flattered and willing.

The premise, for all of the book's unwieldy history, was disarmingly straightforward. My father was eternally fascinated by how things came to be where they currently were. In the case of the automobile entry that he'd repeatedly vowed to co-author with Gerry, he wanted to know where the metal came from, where the leather or vinyl for the seats was manufactured, where the paint came from, the glass, etc. The page would then be cross-referenced so that you could look up a page on paint itself and determine where the chemical components of paint originated, where the particles that formed glass had once been granules of sand, how that sand had been deposited and swept around by ocean currents, based on the best understanding then available. Maps would untuck from each of its opposing pages on whatever cartographic scale was merited, and, spread like wings, would chart the voyages of things, as heroic in my father's mind as the boldest venture in the Age of Exploration.

He'd gone so far as to write up a dust jacket
for the book itself, although leaving enough gaps in
it so that he could, as he phrased it, "put forth his
best stuff when it's all done." The jacket, which he
shared with us as proudly as though it was draped
around an actual book, read thusly:

The Atlas of the Voyages of Things *is a
lavishly illustrated book that documents the
marvelous, intricate, globetrotting chain of
events by which things come to be what and
where they are. It is a book that is somewhat
scholarly in tone, yet addressed to the general
reader. One finds oneself learning that
____originates in _____, that in fact, to one's
amazement, _____ comes from _____, and
that the _____in _____is actually derived
from _____. Anyone, almost anyone—anyone
with the slightest degree of susceptibility to the
specific as it impinges on the universal, or vice-
versa, in short anyone with an iota of curiosity,
will find something to mull over in it. It is
eminently mullworthy. It is decidedly not a book
that one reads straight through—who could bear*

to do so? For to do so would mean that, rather than catching one's breath after learning that _____ is of _____-ian origin, and allowing the ramifications, however great or small, of this discovery to sink in, one would go on in the next breath to learn that ___is of _____. And like some defiance of the principle of res extensa, two bodies (facts) occupying the same space (logical) at once, this would flout all that is harmonious and tolerable.

How narrowly or broadly are "things" to be defined? There is the section on the circulation of fluids in the body, that of the winds known as the Trade Winds, maps of various epidemics, as they are believed to have been transmitted, a map of the spread of languages as they are believed to have emanated out of Africa, or simultaneously in many regions, depending on whether one subscribes to the monogenetic or polygenetic theory of origins. There are maps of the drug trade whose degree of detail might send tremors through the most Kevlar-entrenched drug dealer. There are maps of the genetic modification of foods, delineating how they have sprawled all over

the American landscape, picked up and buffeted
by winds lacking policy agendas. ⟦He updated
some of these over the years, as you have surely
noted.⟧

In short, it is a tome to marvel at, and
to pick up and browse at will. And it has just
arrived on the shelves of the Mid-Manhattan
Library right at 40th Street and Fifth Avenue,
shelved logically under Dewey classification
___._P, ready to be checked out, gaped at, ogled,
handled, caressed, ignored, flung, tiger-charged,
and any of the other innumerable postures
available within the Kama Sutra of the readerly
imagination that books might be seduced into
trying in the middle of the year AD 19_.

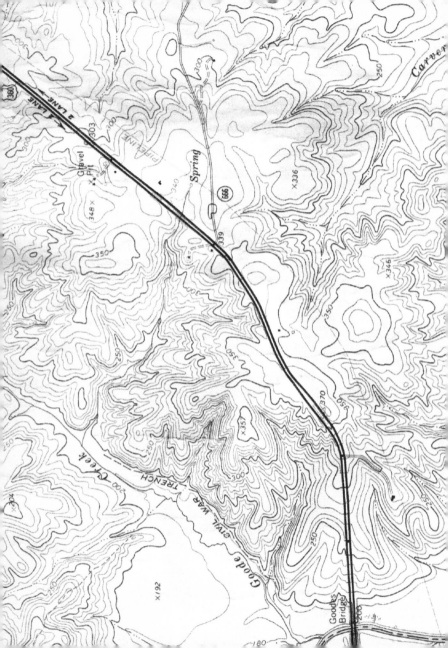

We, too, were part of that collective effort, and felt our responsibility as burden and badge. I can recall a garage sale: neighbors, the Larsens. My mother was picturing their furniture, mentally rearranging it in our house, while my father walked around as if he was at a hands-on museum. He seemed to be particularly drawn by the most impractical items—a battery hold-down for cars that had not been manufactured in decades, a set of binoculars that were unwieldy even for that time. I recall him calling us over, turning the knob of the eyepiece while panning around as he said, "These once belonged to the Margolises, and now I'm going to buy them for a song from the Larsens. And we'll probably hold a garage sale of our own in a few months, at which point hopefully I will dump them off to someone else." He looked sagely at Aidan and me. "You see," he said in a hushed tone, "the way things make their way even around our little neighborhood." I don't recall ever having a garage sale.

Do all families have such unifying themes? And if not, what replaces them? How, otherwise, do they make sense of it all, bring together the noblest and the basest in their histories within a single binding? We were driving to Detroit, once, to see Uncle Gerry. It was the excitement of anticipation—the big city and greasy roadside fare along the way. As we pulled back on the highway after a stop at a diner, my body betrayed me with a riptide of a fart. Aidan immediately began writhing and pinching his nose. He cranked down his window, air rushing into the car. It smelled worse outside, at that moment, in Eastern Michigan. My hair whipping up, I reached over and, his own hand grabbing my arm midway up, wrestled him. I was bigger, stronger—that was before Aidan shot up and overtook me in every physical sense—but he was next to the handle. My

mother's, "Boys, stop that!" could barely be heard
in the melee, when my father's voice roared over
the wind: "Now listen here. We're going to track
that fart for *The Atlas*, by God, Jay. I'm putting
you and Aidan in charge of those pages. And if
anyone's going to open up the window, you'd
better make note of *exactly* where we are!" Yes, we
were reduced to howling laughter, and the fighting
was subdued, but more, that fart became the stuff
of legend. Years later, we'd mime unsuspecting
readers whistling with exaggerated innocence as
they flipped through the pages, and then overacted
scratching of heads, and eventually wide-eyed
horror.

Only later, once my mother had divorced my
father and removed herself several states from
his lingering charms, did I learn that she'd been
skeptical of the book ever seeing the light of day.
And, indeed, her doubt was justified—when
my father eventually went into the hospital, the
complications ensuing from a laryngectomy gouging
his ability to take care of himself even more acutely
than his ability to speak, I was given the charge
of cleaning out his apartment. By this point, he

was headed for assisted living if he made it out of the hospital. As I rummaged through his stuff, mostly books and papers, but also a remarkable collection of rocks, I came upon only bits and traces of anything like a work-in-progress. There were pages and pages of research notes, written out on legal pads and on the blank sides of manuscript pages, and copies of maps with incomprehensible annotations and arrows plunging and swooping about, but nothing that even approximated a coherent text. I tried to keep together anything that I thought might have belonged in *The Atlas*. It turned out that his apartment abounded with as much pornography as geography, and the former made more sense, at least, to one sifting through the detritus of a life lived largely alone. As I worked, I noted the relative heights of the two piles, rooting for *The Atlas* pile, but knowing it would likely be a dead heat.

At various points in what felt like an excavation, I would phone Aidan to discuss what to do with certain items that looked like they might have value—this sterling silver unpromisingly packed in a crushed cardboard carton, a broach that depicted a woman—our grandmother?—in solemn sepias. During these conversations, I felt as though Aidan was making a concerted effort to avoid sounding impatient, and I was made starkly aware of how different we were, how successfully he'd managed to extricate himself from the radius of our father's magnetism. He was a stockbroker in New York, trading in oil futures, and, if his standard of living was any gauge, damned good at it. I was somewhat fascinated by what he did. Sometimes I'd come across a book about Wall Street while contemplating library purchases, and I'd seize the opportunity to consult with him.

"Sure," he'd say. "If someone in Michigan wants to read about the New York financial markets, that sounds as good as anything else."

Sometimes, I was more direct. "What is it that you *do* all day?"

He'd shrug aside the question. "It's not really interesting. Then again, it's not supposed to be. Only type *interest* that matters to my company is percent on the dollar." He had an accent that I otherwise only heard on television and in movies.

It was the same when it came to asking Aidan

about being a parent. His answers were terse; there was the occasional extended anecdote, usually about something "cute," like his daughter's "One-of-Everything" collection, but other than that, minimal info. I liked being able to look things up— that's just my way. As a source, Aidan seemed rich, substantive, and reputable, but was frustratingly lacking in an index.

Like Aidan, my mother had bolted when she saw daylight, I think. The way I'd construed it, after staying in the Midwest to marry him upon graduating college, she must have undergone a sort of Copernican Revolution at some point, realizing she wasn't anywhere near the center of my father's self-contained cosmos. Her own family came from outside Philadelphia, and they welcomed her back until she could relocate with the childhood sweetheart who was conveniently just the other side of a divorce himself. It might have been mere coincidence, just as it might have been coincidence that her geographical proximity to Aidan seemed to correspond to a greater emotional closeness, as was the case, I suppose, with father and me. Then again, her closeness with Aidan may have stemmed from the fact that as a grandmother, as it turned out, she was a natural, a singer of strictly arias. Her disappointment that I wasn't seeing anyone, or anyone worth really talking about for more than a few awkward moments, was ever-palpable; my emphatic recommendations of the latest mysteries that she would love, no matter how right I was, fell ever short.

At some point in the process of sorting through my father's things, I realized that caves and cave-related items were demanding the formation of a third pile. Indeed, this would keep me on my toes—pictures of the interiors of caves bear a striking resemblance to certain close-up treatments of the human body. You see, my father wouldn't go to the hereafter without leaving behind something catalogued in the Library of Congress—after all that, he was an author. GB603.P46, to be exact, or Dewey 551.4P. I haven't memorized these systems, no, though they are our Periodic Tables. When I was getting my library science degree, there was a period in which if you handed me a book, I could have turned it over a couple of times, scanning its exterior only, and spit out a pretty reasonable guess as to where exactly it would be shelved. Nowadays, I've only retained those that stir specific passions.

The book, *Spelos: An Ode to Caves*, had been available at the local store for a while, propped above the handwritten sign proudly proclaiming, "Local Author Gus Pardo!!!!!!!" but the copy there never budged more than an inch or two. It got slightly dog-eared over the years, its pages turning creamy and mottled—when he self-published, my father did not know to use paper that would withstand time and other elements. The real moment it hit me with desolation was when I held it aloft, once, and noted a fresh smudge. That fingerprint looked, at a certain angle, like slime creeping its way out of the cave entrance that graced the cover. When I saw the smeared copy, I thought about buying it at the local store, but somehow it seemed like in the small town where we lived it would cause too much commotion— Sam, the guy who ran the bookstore, knew my dad well, and would surely ask him, "Hey, why's your *son* buying your book, Gus?"

But the copy of *Spelos* that was housed in our

nation's capital was another story. I remember visiting Washington D.C. with the family, when Aidan was thirteen and I sixteen, and making our way to the glorious Library amidst the other palatial buildings, as they seemed to my decidedly Midwestern sensibility. I remember spending much of the three days we spent there bedazzled, in awe of dimensions, buildings that appeared to have been stretched out like the limousines we saw on the streets, and brightness that seemed to dance off every surface. My mother had to yell out my name a couple of times in intersections, and Aidan premiered the "jay-walking" jokes that immediately entered the permanent database of obnoxious family references.

Our stop at the Library of Congress was surely one of the highlights of that trip. Our father kept announcing that there were "thousands of miles of books" there, adding, "That's more than the distance that we traveled to get here." I remember my mother shaking her head—she really wanted more facetime with the seats of power: the Capitol, the White House, the Monument; for her, the LC was a glorious architectural specimen, but, at the end of the day, just a library. My father's insistence that it really was "the library *of* Congress" seemed to carry some appeal for her—she thought she might spot a congressperson. Once there, we got the needed special permission to go back into the stacks, as Aidan and I were technically too young. My dad even half-joked with the guard that they had better reserve a slot, "yea wide and yea high," for the atlas he was eventually to finish; he actually, as I recall, apologized for making them wait.

Finally, after various delays, we located the book. Unlike the much-handled version in the bookstore back home, this copy had had its cover stripped, and the black spine declaring the title in gold lettering seemed more hardened, as though it had gone off to join the military and been forced to toughen up, gather an austere dignity. And the very cataloguing itself was revelatory for me. The transition between Dewey and LC is a conversion accomplished in seconds with a computer program nowadays, but I can still remember marveling at the unfamiliar codes on the books as we strode through, which seemed like intimations of an adult world I could barely glimpse, tantalizingly and dauntingly complicated.

Of course, we had always had copies sitting
around in the house—since it was self-published,
he got more than the customary ten copies or
whatever it is that an author receives. Oddly
enough, while over the years I'd opened it many
times, and read many pages, I'd never read the
book straight through from start to finish. I knew
it was about caves, of course, and that it was about
more than caves, too. That in its 137 pages, my
father had captured a passion for going into caves
that had flourished in the years before I'd been
born. That he'd mused on their natural history,
their flora and fauna, their dankness and darkness,
their labyrinthine souls. He'd touched on sleep
cycles, prehistoric aesthetics, philosophy, oracles,
blindness. (His eclecticism and the solipsism of
self-published work, less common then, threw the
cataloguers, Deweyan and LC alike, for a loop; I
knew based on my dips in that they'd probably
gotten it wrong.) He'd gotten a cult following
among spelunkers, a cult if ever there was one,
judging by the occasional fan mail that he received,
sometimes bearing the name of a cave as its return

address ("Funny guy, this one!"), which he would share with us boomingly over the dinner table. "This guy, I've got to get him to do a section of *The Atlas*," he'd say on occasion if he got a particularly eccentric letter, let's say one featuring a handwritten map of a set of caverns.

It was written when I was an infant, and so from the time I was young it was sort of always around. But quickly I'd long passed the point where it had been assumed that we had all read it—I know Aidan lapped me in this regard—and so as often as I urged myself to do so, it seemed that the other, more urgent reading material kept piling up. First there was high school, then college, where I studied literature, which certainly didn't leave me a whole lot of time to catch up on such back-reading. And then, on to a library science degree, where the reading was much more technical and technologically oriented than anything I'd encountered before, demanding a whole new way of reading. It was the beginning of the heyday of the Internet; suddenly bibliophilia was just another trait among many that qualified one to be a top-notch librarian, and even those of us who put books first had to embrace "information management."

I was familiar enough with the book that I could carry on the small talk that usually circulated around the it—it wasn't as though spelunkers were making pilgrimages to Esoch, Michigan, where I got my first library job, or anything of that nature. Mostly, friends and relatives would make reference to it, and occasionally, a woman that I was seeing. Somehow, none of them ever got past the first question, "What's it about?" My stock answer, "It's all about caves...it's hard to describe, though, because it's not *just* about the actual, physical cave," was more than sufficient for them. Part of me, perhaps the part that had always yearned to be a fiction writer instead of a librarian who nonetheless trafficked so often in fictions, would itch to say more, to make it up, to conjure a version of what I thought the book was about based on my skimmings and perusals over the years. Another part of me, though, was relieved that I didn't have to lie about something so fundamental to how I thought about my family. Not even the biggest wiseass I dated, Erica—six months—would press me: "Well, what's the first *sentence*, at least?" No, come to think of it, Erica would have been more ruthless still, would have asked about the *last* sentence. Glad she never got around to it.

At the Esoch Library, I put in an order for a copy right away. The head librarian was more than glad to do so. "Well, of course, it's your father's book," she said, positively tickled to have the son of a bona fide local author join the staff. Later, I moved to Biltchrist and ordered a copy there, too. There, Lucy, the reference librarian, ruled the nonfiction order with an iron fist. She was less than enthusiastic about ordering a copy, less game to do so on a whim, suspicious that I was trying to slip something past her. A bulldog of a woman, she'd intimidated me from day one.

"Are there any reviews of it I could read?" she inquired.

I thought about the reviews I knew of. One in the local paper in Esoch, where I'd grown up, written by a guy who was posed in several fishing photos on my dad's walls. I knew him as the shorter guy, in height somewhere between my father and the dangling fish. A couple of write-ups in spelunking magazines, which were, believe it or not, obscure. Not a whimper in *Publishers Weekly* or *Library Journal* or *Book Trade*, the sources that Lucy relied upon with an almost-religious fervor, and that we were expected to swear by also. Not even a blurb in *Outside* or anywhere with journalistic cachet or popular standing.

"I think I can get ahold of some fan mail from some readers," I tried. She thought I was kidding. "Yes, well, bring in whatever *reviews* you have." In that moment, I made a mental vow not to be so slavishly bound to the serendipities and stratagems of the marketplace when I had the opportunity, to seek out the obscure and the overlooked.

The copy I brought in wound up on the shelf. That was okay—at that time, my dad didn't need the $14.95 plus shipping and handling that he was charging for it, but years later, sitting in his hospital room, I thought, Medicare and health insurance notwithstanding, we could both use it now.

In that very hospital room, I was caught red-handed for never having read *Spelos*. One day I was confronted by, of all people, a nurse named

Desireé, to whom my father had apparently talked about the book. She was making small talk with me, a better diversion than the paper, while he was asleep, and she was tending to him, cleaning, etc.

"So, is it true he's written a book?" She was wise to confirm, as the greatest, most jarring post-operative complication had been, of course, a form of delirium. His connection with reality came and went unpredictably, and of course there was no mechanism yet sensitive enough to detect it, unlike the more autonomic functions.

"Indeed it is," I said. "He's not making that up."

"So how does it feel to be the son of a writer?"

"Oh," I said, "it's an honor, I suppose."

She smiled. "Tell me about the book he's written again?"

I led with the standard line, but she wasn't going anywhere. She scrubbed his arm.

"Well, what about caves, then, if not the actual physical caves?"

I stumbled. I think I stammered something about the deeper meaning in caves. Something about going deeper, the way you could venture into caves. I felt as though among the machines in the room was a bullshit detector whose needle was flailing in the red zone.

"Hmmm, sounds interesting," she murmured, cocking an eyebrow. It was unmistakable—she *knew* that I was a cheat. That night, I yanked it almost angrily off the shelf where it had been gathering dust; people always expect a librarian's home shelves will somehow be immune to residue, and speech immune to clichés, but neither is the case. Thus I began to plow through it. One hundred thirty-seven pages in a matter of hours, and the sense that my father's soul was once, perhaps still was, magma, lit and surging.

The next time I was there, another nurse was on call, but about a week later I overlapped with Desireé again. "Hello," I said.

My father was conscious, now. He did not speak much, for he couldn't, but his whisper still had a robustness to it.

"Hey," I said. "About my father's book, you know, that we were talking about last time?"

"Mmmmm."

"Since you expressed curiosity," I said. "I brought a copy. In case you were interested in reading it." It was checked out under my own name from the Biltchrist Public Library.

My father spotted as much immediately. He said, "You check out library? *Your*?" He left out words that he felt he didn't need.

"I did, I did," I said.

"What if someone needs?" he said.

I couldn't quite gauge where he was vis-à-vis reality. I said, "That's true, but it will be due back in three weeks." I gestured to Desireé, "And I'm sure Desireé won't hang on to it longer than that." She nodded in affirmation. I didn't have the heart to tell him that as far as I knew, the book had never left the library. Perhaps it had, but I certainly had never checked it out to anyone.

A few minutes went by. Then he squinted at me, "What is it you do...the library?"

"I'm the Director of Circulation," I said.

He paused for a moment, stared out at the wall across from the bed, from where sometimes the Hula-hoop girl emerged. She was nowhere near now. Then he asked a question I was not quite expecting, yet somehow dreading. "Who else checked it out? When?"

It was indeed one of the older books, old enough that it still had the pocket in the back where a card had once designated the due dates of the book. Any book up until a certain point wore its history on its sleeve, its record of encounters, its promiscuity or chasteness. Only in high school libraries was there an actual signature; for public libraries, a date stamp did the trick. I peered in the pocket, just to be sure. Those cards had been discarded with the advent of the computerized system. For a period of time those records had been recorded and archived electronically, but after the Patriot Act, many librarians, myself included, were wary about this government—I am tempted to use the word "regime"—meddling in the privacy of our patrons. We've felt tested by this possibility: we've become versed in the Privacy Act to an unprecedented degree, and I know many of us who have responded by destroying checkout records with a newfound urgency. There is no way to tell who has checked out many of our books and when, and there is no way to know for sure that this book has never left the library.

More likely it has sat on the shelf next to

its companions growing old, peering out at the movements of patrons, sizing them up perhaps just as readily as they are sized up. Yes, I know it sounds strange—you might conclude that I, and not my father, was the one suffering from delirium, but I have occasionally tried to take the perspective of the books on my shelves, imagining that they choose their recipients as much as they are chosen. Like animals in the wild, they can, I suppose, camouflage themselves such that at times they blend in with their surroundings as readily as a tree frog, hugging the walls of the shelves around them, appearing less palatable than the plump bestseller they lean against. Or like abandoned puppies in pet stores—I was going to say prostitutes, but fear it could single-handedly shatter your impression of me, and perhaps I, like these books, can only hope to make an impression— they can poke themselves out just a bit further than the nearest competitor, jutting forth an irresistible moist black nose between pouting eyes.

These are fanciful notions, of course, and who is to say which is the stranger phenomenon in the Grand View—Man Seeking Book, or Book Seeking

Man? And why not a mutual wooing?

I glanced down into the pocket anyway, indeed empty. My father is a man who would have cared deeply about the Patriot Act and its implications for American citizens, privacy, and freedom. But instead of going into that, I told a half-truth, a truth that five years earlier would have been intact. I said, "We have that information on the computer now, dad."

He nodded. Desireé took the book, thanked me. Said the last book she read was months ago. These hospital shifts are killing her.

One of the most striking stories I read when I was in college was Borges's "Library of Babel," and on occasion I have thought myself the proprietor of that very library. Borges's fictional library is a metaphysical marvel, a library that essentially comprises the whole of the universe— the universe *as* library. Its volumes are random and contain every possible permutation of text, from gibberish to the complete works of Shakespeare. Within the library that Borges conjures, not only is every book ever written shelved somewhere, but every *possible* book is shelved, every conceivable configuration of the alphabet. The conceit is too dizzying to think about for very long, but it serves as a good antidote to certain fundamental realities:

funds are limited, books go unread, tumble out
of print, serve as doorstops—all too effectively, I
might add; the greatest libraries of civilizations
burn down, suns collapse, abandon planets without
child support. And each life is limited—there is
only so much reading that one can consume in the
course of a lifetime, and the guests are waiting
for the ham. No, that's my brother Aidan's life,
and his line, too—once we were speaking in his
bedroom, and he was expressing concern for me,
my solitude, the dearth of female companionship
in my life. I had just broken off an apparently
blossoming relationship shortly before coming for
Thanksgiving. At some point, despite my brother's
better intentions, it became apparent that there
was nothing more to be said—we could both hear
the mirth below, the hubbub of Aidan's kids and
those of the neighbors who were over, the clatter
of dishes being hoisted from the kitchen to prime
spots on the table, sloshing sauce. And Aidan, at
last, smiling at the futility of his words: "Well, the
guests are waiting for the ham."

Desireé had called and warned me he wasn't doing well, that he seemed less cognizant of his surroundings. He was talking about Lake Superior and hunting lodges and a mother bear. She said that by the way she had read the book, and while she wasn't sure she had understood most of it, and it was unlike any other book that she had ever read, she found it to be "powerful and very, very emotional." I thanked her without quite knowing why, and added, "I bet he'd be glad to know that."

She said, "Oh, I told him. I particularly told him I liked the part about bats."

"Oh, yes," I shot right back, perhaps a bit too eagerly. "Where he goes into the whole thing about insideness and outsideness, and how we are becoming more bat-like as we spend more and more of our lives indoors."

"Yes." I could hear her smiling over the phone as she noted that I had read it, perhaps concurrently with her. "I could identify with that. I *never* seem to get outside these days." She paused for a moment. "Some of that stuff was strange, though."

"The stuff about the proportions of the bat's head to its body?"

"That's it," she said, and I could sense her nodding and even laughing.

"My dad's a strange guy," I said. "He has some strange notions about the world."

So later, when I arrived at the hospital, and Desireé had left the book behind with a note, he came awake. He couldn't really gesture, lacking the facial control to do so, but I could sense that inwardly he was motioning to it as he said, "She liked it."

"So I hear."

Then, a few minutes later, "Who'll have it next?"

I said, "I'll bring it back to the library."

"Hmm. Then?"

"It will go back on the shelf."

"Then?"

At what point does one recognize that the truth is precisely the wrong instrument for a task? I was in charge of circulation. A slowness, a quasi-geological time governs the circulation of books: the punctuation of frantic movements as a book takes on a buzz, gets reviewed, followed by years of stillness, silence, neglect. Perhaps a motion picture is commissioned, produced, released; the book stirs, reenters the commerce of the world, mingles and becomes inebriated in the gala of its success, and eventually tapers off, only somewhat-reluctantly, into a second retirement. Envision a remake thirty years later—it happens. There is always hope, you see.

But imagine if one could speed up time, fast-forward and rewind over longer intervals, see at once all the permutations of a book's lifetime. From this vantage point, the Director of Circulation might appear the ringleader of a circus—coordinating acrobats, elephants, fire-breathing ladies, third-rate clowns, contract renegotiations. Books would fly off the shelves in a blur, leaving gaps like children's debut teeth, making their forays out into the world, and swooping back to their perches eventually like osprey. Indeed, sideways and spines-up with their covers spread out, would they look like anything other than birds? I paused, though, as I realized that what was missing from this vision was the temporary habitations of the book outside, its journeys through the neighborhood. Or, as I knew all too well from the day-to-day job, throughout the *world*. How laughably common is it to hear, "I returned that—I'm absolutely positive!" only to receive a sheepish note from a return address far away—New Mexico?—that reads, "*This* turned up while unpacking. Sorry!" One would have hoped for a jar of salsa, at least.

I thought, inevitably, of that Other Book. *The Atlas.* Unwritten, perhaps unwriteable. I pictured the ideal version of that book; once one has admitted the impossible, one might as well usher in its unruly companions. Picture a tracer placed in the book that would record its travels to-and-fro. No, too much of a concession to the regime. Rather, render a version of the book itself including a sheaf of blank pages and empty maps. These would be pages reserved for the recording of the book's own journey, not merely where it went, but what went on in the lives of those around it while it was in their abode. I foresee, and you do too, that gradually the journal grows and grows till it subsumes the book, essentially *becomes* the book. Worry about that then.

I was the Director of Circulation. I said, "It is checked out by a boy."

He seemed pleased with this answer. But not satisfied. Perhaps he, too, at that moment was thinking of *The Atlas*; perhaps he never ceased thinking of it; perhaps it was error to think that it *was* a book at all; perhaps it was rather the very medium of thought itself. "And then?" The machines pulsed and bleeped, the room waited for more. The Hula-hoop froze, though did not tumble—it hovered round the waist of the girl— did I neglect to mention that she was there?

I continued, "He needed it for school." It was all I could think of. The hoop was still poised. "For earth science class."

He laughed. "Required text?" he said.

My father didn't mind imaginative leaps, but he was no Pangloss. "Nope," I said. "For extra credit." The story pushed on. With these minimal legs, it somehow staggered to its feet, however awkwardly. "They're...not covered in the regular curriculum. The teacher...gave them a list. 'Topics Not Covered,' it read. Passed it around the room." Somehow with the contrivance of that list, the story started to plod forward in my mind, then to lumber forth with increased momentum as the sheet worked its way around the room. I didn't know where any of these images, which had the materiality and authority of memories, were coming from, except in the vaguest sense. I could see my father was transfixed. "The kid, he signed up first... for avalanches. He wanted avalanches, desperately. Who wouldn't? He was overjoyed when the list came around...and the four people ahead of him hadn't signed up for avalanches. What were the odds?

"So he signs his name. But when the list comes around and the teacher wants to double-check...she reads off Billy Fletcher's name for avalanches. He

46

wants to protest—he can see from where he's sitting that Billy crossed his name...it's Heath—he... gets mocked for it sometimes, especially next year when they're doing *Macbeth*, anyway it's crossed, blatantly, out, but Billy's bigger, more developed, works out, football player. So Heath keeps his mouth shut. Caves is left, still. Anybody want caves? He shoots up his hand. He *needs* the extra credit way more than he needs avalanches. He's fallen behind, barely passing the class. He doesn't mind earth science, rather enjoys it actually, but it's...a *lot* of memorization. Doesn't have time. Most of his free time is spent over in...the hunting store where he works, helps out his dad, exhausting.

"So he gets one day off, the start of actual hunting season. Everything's closed but...for some reason the library's open. Let's say...the librarian there is anti-hunting. Heath heads for the library and finds your book on caves. Takes it out. Takes out a couple of other books. But he knows the project has to be good. He doesn't have a lot of time, though—next day it's back to the store. He's strapped in math class, too, where Mrs. Clayman is going over the Cartesian graphs. He doesn't get functions. So...he copies a bit, more than a bit, in truth, three pages."

As I related this, a part of me was observing myself, and that part wanted to discern where the details were coming from. They seemed conjured from anywhere and nowhere at once, at first trickling, then gushing forth as though from some reservoir of necessity. A thought which I had vaguely had before crystallized in my mind: nonfiction could be pinned down, assigned its plot of shelf real estate where it could reliably be located in the continuum of knowledge, in any library in any country in the world. But fictions were like transient, shifty renters—all we could do with them was alphabetize them by the arbitrary condition of the author's last name and hope they stayed put.

"So," my father murmured. "He get away with it?"

The tip of my tongue rooted around between my lip and the top of my gums as I pondered, as though the answer was wedged there like food caught in teeth. It was a good question, and it felt like any answer was irrevocable; somehow, too, the answer needed to be dictated by the book. "He gets caught...when his teacher asks him about the part about 'uterine walls.' The class snickers...so she knows it is her professional duty to do something, and when she confronts him, Heath is stymied, tongue-tied." I paused for a moment here. My dad was not Pollyannaish, but why I had been lured into such a cynical cavern of possibility, a seeming dead end? Somehow, glancing over at his sallow cheeks, I felt I needed to push around this.

It came to me all at once, and I said it as quickly as though I was on a fading phone connection. "But he will read the book later for a literature class and understand it much more and look back in disgust and pathos on his younger ways. And he will write his college essay on the book and the whole experience, and it will get him into his second choice."

I looked over at my father; he appeared to be in something akin to a trance. As for me, I'd gotten so caught up in the story that I didn't even see Desireé come into the room.

"This is what happens next to the book...," I explained, as if this explanation would make sense to her. But if it didn't, I shrugged, so be it; I'd realized something that my father, perhaps, had already known, that delirium was a form of understanding.

As Desireé crouched over him to give him his medication, he said, "We are cave people," perhaps by way of his own explanation. Somehow, the words were comedic and weighty at once. Neither of us responded, except by smiling, which seemed about right.

Afterward, as I drove home, I retraced my story as though I had just surfaced from a particularly vivid dream, trying to figure out from whence its ingredients had grown, by what recipe it had been put together. I had dated a woman once who was a high school teacher, who had told me a couple of stories about plagiarists that she had caught; I hadn't thought about her recently. The other details—avalanches, buff football players— seemed like miracles.

The next evening, I told him about the couple that had checked the book out next. Somehow, a fragment set me off—something I heard about once on NPR? "They're a couple that is getting married in a cave. She's an archaeologist; he's a dean at the school where she works. She has a vision of a splendid wedding that actually will be set in a cave—hundreds of candles illuminating the lush walls, dripping sounds in the background, chains of flowers lining the mantle that happens to run along the cave's contours, a photographer who must crane his neck around stalactites.

"The groom, the dean, he's a little stiff, but he decides to go along with it. She's brought out so many wonderful aspects of him—spontaneity, adventure—that he can't complain. They get out books about caves, look for 'Cave Readings.' *Spelos* looks promising, looks like it was written for that target audience of brides and grooms looking for pithy cave quotes. Doing his part, dutifully, he reads the passage on bats, somehow panics. It's not about the bats, it's about something deeper that she represents, someplace she's leading him. Too much. Soon, for consecutive nights, he's having dreams, nightmares, bats swarming.

"They split up. She marries a local chef who is delighted to get married in a cave. They have a cave-aged cheese spread at the wedding that rivals anything anyone's ever seen.

"He neglects to return the book. Pining for her, he clings to it, a remnant of that relationship, what once was, even though it is too painful to actually read it.

"Then one day, he meets a new girl. Everything's great—she loves the symphony and the opera. It's what he's always imagined. A couple of years go by. They are moving...to New Mexico, of all places. He's a little bit wary but hears the Santa Fe Symphony is fantastic. As they are packing up, she turns up the book, which is absurdly overdue at this point. She can't believe he hasn't returned it. Not only that, but she knows that he was previously all but married in a cave, and she's savvy—she actually puts two and two together; she interprets the reasons for the book's continued presence there and continued absence from the library all-too-accurately. They fight—about other last-minute scrambles, the need to return the cable box, et cetera—she never lets on that she sees the significance of it, besides its being long overdue. He doesn't quite understand why she wants him to return it *immediately*—they are in the middle of rolling lamps in bubble-wrap—but he does. Dutiful. At first they want to charge him at the library but the librarian is in a light-hearted mood and clears the fine when he explains the situation. The librarian sleeps well that night, thinking of him as she is drifting off.

"The book is back but it's not there for long. There is a woman who has been taking a class in the evening." I looked up; I had been so immersed in the story that I had forgotten the presence of my audience. I glanced over at him. He was fast asleep, his snoring steady and serene.

The next night, I told the story of the woman. The stories continued to unfold over the next several nights. Sometimes Desireé was present, and sometimes not. I had never told stories before—it felt exhilarating. I would leave and pick up my car and pay the ticket at the gate, imagining SCHEHERAZADE on a vanity plate—how could you pare it down to six characters and still make it recognizable? Immediately I reprimanded myself for being so flippant—my father was on his deathbed, and I was hardly saving my own life. Or was I?

I thought about Aidan reading his children stories, and I wondered if I would be any good at it.

My father had seen and experienced enough of the world that that there was very little I would bite my tongue about with him; almost anything that popped into my head would be fair game. But if you were telling stories to children you would have to limit what you could say. Did you just make exotic dishes with minimal ingredients, or were the expectations lower for items ordered off the children's menu? When I'd visited Aidan in New York, I'd always been anxious about bedtime—it seemed like a nightly trial, a forum in which all of your shortcomings and neuroses as a parent and as a person would be showcased. Were you a pushover, or were you "just not the creative type," or, perhaps worse, too preoccupied with budgets and deadlines to suspend disbelief even fleetingly— your own and another's—in outspoken mice and yawning moons?

I would wait downstairs nervously thumbing the remote through cable channels, gnawed at by the sense that I should be doing something to help, something to make the night special because I was there. Meanwhile, I'd let Aidan and Jen tend to those duties, like any other night. Eventually, they would rejoin me, shaking their heads, swapping a detail or two about their ordeals, and every so often glancing at the head of the stairs, looking for the pajama-clad figure they hoped would not appear. Next time I was out at Aidan's, I vowed, I would volunteer for bedtime services.

For now, though, I was in the thicker woods of the adult story-world. "It's an adult ed class. She's getting her life back on track after a series of abusive or nondescript relationships. Doing something good for the soul.

"Needless to say, she develops a crush on her handsome thirtysomething teacher, who has been ushering her into the realm of philosophy—the class is called 'The Moderns on the Ancients,' or maybe it's 'The Ancients on the Moderns,' whatever. She shoots him glances; he might or might not be responding, but she confirms her initial impression that he isn't wearing a ring.

"After she *finally* gets her grade in the mail— she did just fine—she musters up the courage to call him and ask him out. He is surprisingly appreciative and charmingly awkward all at once, and says it would be great to go out for dinner sometime. He tells her that her paper on Nietzsche on Plato was great, and that he was just surprised that she made no mention of Plato's Allegory of the Cave—apologizes that they never had time for it on the syllabus but surely she's read it. She hasn't? Oh, he tells her that oh, she must.

"She goes to the library immediately, and locates the Platonic dialogues. There's nothing there that even looks cave-related, just a bunch of Greek names: *Meno, Crito*, no *Cavo*. Disheartened, she heads for the computer and looks up caves—maybe it's nestled next to other cave books, maybe there's an *Anthology of Cave Literature*; she'll try "allegory" last. She goes to the cave shelf—the 551s—and there, lo and behold, is something called *Spelos: An Ode to Caves*. The book seems to be beckoning to her—it all but has Plato's autograph on it.

"She reads 137 pages in one fell swoop. There are references throughout the volume to Plato's myth, but they're oblique, scattered like clues. Over dinner, she says something about bats and the sizes of their heads relative to their bodies—he hears 'hats,' though, and finds the comment crass and dull. She senses his boredom and the disparity of their intellects.

"After he drops her off, she takes the book, which was in her purse, and flings it off a bridge where it flips over three times and hurtles into the back of a flatbed filled with gravel and dust. It rains a bit; the book is partly sheltered. The next morning, the driver picks it up and brings it back to the library. It's the last day of the library book sale, and he gets three children's books about construction and trucks dirt cheap, and brings them home to his kids and is proud because it is his profession and they will be readers.

"But he's brought it to the wrong library—the name got slightly obscured by the rain, and he brought it to the library one town over. As they attempt to check it in, of course, they recognize that. And they do what they always do *in these cases.*

"They send it to the 'Greenvale' in the next state over, because there are two Greenvales within thirty miles of each other and this happens all the time.

"Well, at this point the book is a little bit tattered, a little bit scruffy. When it arrives at the Greenvale, Indiana Public Library, they roll their eyes a bit, re-label it, figuring that at some fundamental level all the libraries of the world are united—head librarian there fancies herself a bit of a socialist, anyhow. So they treat it like a new book; it spends a week at the bindery.

"When it hits the shelves again, they put it on display as a new book, really an understandable error, because it is shimmering in its new packaging. It happens that a man who has recently been diagnosed with obsessive-compulsive disorder has recently had a major breakthrough after years of therapy and failed remedies. His therapist has recommended that rather than attempting to beat his obsessions by avoiding them, he needs to find an outward focus *for* his obsessive energy, an object worthy of affection. He cites Freud; the patient is game.

"He heads to the library immediately and hits the New Nonfiction shelves, then plunges into the older books. He pulls down four or five, each of which seems to promise a lifetime, or at least many months, of promising obsessional material. He clutches a stack and heaves it on the circulation desk up front: a book on kites and kite-making, one on mutual funds, one on the Civil War, one on stargazing, and all of them balancing on the slenderest of the bunch, the afterthought he has grabbed on spelunking."

At this point, I'd taken to actually plotting and writing up the scenarios the night before. Having never composed fiction before, I'd grown restless in the evening hours, thinking about where the book would go next. At first I wrote simply in order to sleep, but it also seemed as though the stories would be more meaningful for him, since he'd been such a reader himself throughout his life, but didn't have the fine motor control needed to operate a book at this point. As for the oral tradition, I could always embellish in the moment of performance, too. I could not quite discern pride in his minimal responses; his gestural repertoire was confined to the eyes and the muscles around the orbits at this point, but I felt that he couldn't be disappointed at my stabs at writing. I wrote about my OCD patient:

"When he reads it, though, he reads with fervor. He's a Dostoyevskian reader, and though that could mean many things, in his case, it means that he reads in the manner in which he imagines

that Dostoyevsky wrote—ravenous, staggering
through his dimly lit apartment clutching the
book, luminous with something teetering between
ecstasy and epilepsy, ingesting swathes of prose
in desperate gulps, like an infant born undersized,
suckling harder. When once he misplaces the book
and locates it at last, after a forty-minute search,
concealed under an errant cushion, he collars it
like a treacherous friend; he is at once too furious
and too attached to reprimand for long. It goes
without saying that he takes it into the bathroom,
and sometimes loses himself on the porcelain
seat as though this was the most natural reading
position, as if reading was only one part of *that*.
His bathroom, anyway, overlooks an alley fraught
with the stink and presence of people, and when
he is reading the book it is summer, thus windows
are wide open and the whole building seems to be
singing, a chorus of vague suggestions and clashing
soloists. He devours it like a novel, fastening on
the dramas of the explorers, their obsessions with
going further and with firsts—the first to conquer
a particular cave or to prove, slithering on their
stomachs, that two caves were ultimately connected

in some remote channel inaccessible to all but those who were willing to die for an idea, the idea that all things must be connected.

"At some point in the bathroom a slight but terrible thing happens; he drops the book onto the toilet seat. He grabs as though it is his only pair of glasses tumbling over the railing of an ocean-liner, and manages to rescue the book from tumbling in, but for a brief moment it lands unmistakably on the toilet seat. Disgusting, to him. More than that, it sends him spiraling into thoughts, thoughts that only an obsessive would have—how many other times might this book have landed near toilets, been handled by germ-laden people, people with no regard for hygiene whatsoever, and no regard for the fact that this book will be read by the purer and more innocent, oblivious to its former depravities? Reason returns momentarily—he recalls that it is a New Book, glistening, can only have been checked out once or twice, but then *what to think of these other books?* Now the thought has taken up lodging—it is too late to unthink it, and he can't shake it. He cannot even bring himself to handle the other books, not even to bring them back. He tells his friend, who knows about his condition. His friend, ever-loyal, aware and sympathetic toward his condition, will return them—he makes a joke: put the kite book on a string and read it at arm's length. As his friend departs with the books, the obsessive actually considers this as a possibility for future library excursions.

"The friend returns most of the books. But the cave book seems special, somehow. He decides to re-check it out under his own name. Is so provoked by its magnificent descriptions and reflections that he decides to try spelunking. He brings it—pocket-sized, it isn't exactly going to do any lasting damage to his back."

Have you forgotten, for even an instant, as I must admit I had, that these stories were meant for my father, that he was listening all along? Indeed, he had passed away at some point during my reading of this last story, which thus never was told. Little in his features distinguished this latest placidity from that sleep which had become our ritual, our agreement. I found it hard to believe that there wouldn't be another story tomorrow.

With some trepidation, that evening I phoned my mother to inform her of the news. I was almost relieved when her voice betrayed sorrow, perhaps a mourning for some ineradicable part of herself, though her words were no more than, "Well, I'm deeply glad you could be there for him."

The funeral was later that week. Aidan and his wife and the kids flew in, Gerry, and even Desireé made an appearance with her son—it was oddest to see her in black instead of her nurse's attire. A chilly, rainy day, flood warnings. The flash storms were made more dramatic by the flatness all around; Aidan's children would remember the Midwest as strung up by lightning throughout their lives. Afterward, everyone came over to my place, the profusion of voices and bodies like armor against the cataclysm without.

But afterward, left alone in my apartment, I felt as though something was still unresolved. It was selfish, I knew: my story had been prematurely cut off. I knew, at least by reputation, of a set of caves, nearly a day's drive away, but I was the Director of Circulation, after all, and my father had just passed away, and so I could take some time off.

Into the mouth of one of the caves I plunged, the copy of the book borne in one hand, flashlight in the other illuminating the walls. I was mindful of my father's own words in *Spelos*—at the spot you needed light most in a cave, you could never quite get it: right where your head would eventually, no matter how careful and experienced you were, knock into an unexpected lintel of rock. I didn't have a helmet, but the book made a good temporary stand-in.

The immediate sensation was coldness, a roaming cold that shook free of the walls and crept around, the kind you get standing shoulder-deep in a lake under passing clouds. There was a cave-smell, too, like wet pavement, only slightly metallic. Once I had my bearings, I could understand "mouth" more viscerally; the interior was like the ominous pictures of periodontal disease that hang on dentist's walls. Rock-spears oozed like fleshy icicles, and the glazed walls glittered with what looked like sugar residue in a downed mug of coffee—what an onslaught of detail in those walls, and what a staggering thought that without illumination, they would remain forever invisible, inaccessible.

After several false leads, I found a crevice in
an overhang. It seemed as though the likelihood
of it being disturbed back here was slim. I wedged
myself upward and thrust my body in the direction
that my light revealed this slight opening. My
shoulders found themselves between two walls,
as though I was being held by the cave. This was
mildly comforting, and I paused to savor it, but
at once felt a twinge of danger—a few feet away,
these same walls, angled slightly closer, could
crush. I reached out and with a flick of the wrist,
sent the book off into the darkness, then retreated.

Checking it back into the library system
in a few days would require little other than a
passworded function override, and the records
would, of course, be swept clean in a couple of
weeks. If anyone ever sought it, it would be tagged
"MISSING" and the usual searches would ensue; I'd
go through the motions, use it as an opportunity
to look for fresh mouse droppings. I had no idea
what fate would befall the book itself. Would the
temperature of the cave preserve its molecular
structure like fine cheese, or would dampness eat
away at it, inviting microorganisms to feast upon

its pages, cannibalize descriptions of their own likenesses? Would an intrepid spelunker eventually stumble across it and send it back, or see it as a sign and take it to the next cave on his itinerary?

As I decided to depart, then, pitch darkness at my back, I felt that whatever future lay before his book, it would be safer here, more permanent even than in the Library of Congress itself, more faithful to my father's ultimate ambition. And surely it was self-delusion, but I'd driven all that day fueled by coffee and a vision: the words and the *Ding an sich* of the cave reaching out, embracing each other. In the embrace, whether eternal embalming or disintegration into cave sludge, I'd felt sure I would sense both what had created me and what would ultimately end me. En route, I'd pictured it cinematically, as sculpture, as jewelry; the reality was less dramatic, and now even that was gone.

For a moment, though, I risked flicking off the lamp. It was the sheerest darkness I could recall, and I instantly lost track of my limbs. I knew I needed to steer myself with arms extended; I knew the fingers of my left hand were still poking through the handle of the flashlight and my right

palm was fully splayed. It was a directionless dark
in which I could still distinguish degrees of cold
but not myself. I kept expecting to smack into
something, almost willing it to happen, because
I'd lost all recollection of pain, of sensation. Not
wishing to push my luck, I flicked the light back on
to exit—I'd gone only a yard or so.

I took in the cave one last time. Its shadows
were restless, already arranging themselves into
the stories I'd carry to Aidan's kids, much like the
ones I might one day tell my own. As I neared the
mouth, children's voices were audible just outside.
Abruptly, I re-entered at once light, warmth,
clamor. At first it was too much—I threw the hand
with the lamp straight up to shield my eyes, but
the other remained stubbornly outstretched as I
pointed myself in the direction where I recalled the
parking lot to be. I could feel my skin awakening
to the moist air. With each step blinking my way
back, I gradually lowered the lamp. It was tougher
in daylight, but I wanted to see how long I could
maintain that feeling of open, open arms.

About the Author

Tim Horvath received his MFA from the University of New Hampshire, where he won the Thomas Williams Memorial Prize. His story "The Understory" won the 2006 Raymond Carver Short Story Award, judged by Bill Henderson, and in 2008 he received a Yaddo fellowship. His work has appeared in or is forthcoming in *Alimentum: The Literature of Food*, *Fiction*, *Web Conjunctions*, *Puerto del Sol*, and many other journals. He lives in New Hampshire with his wife and daughter, and works as a psychiatric counselor and a creative writing instructor.